The Wonderful World of Math!

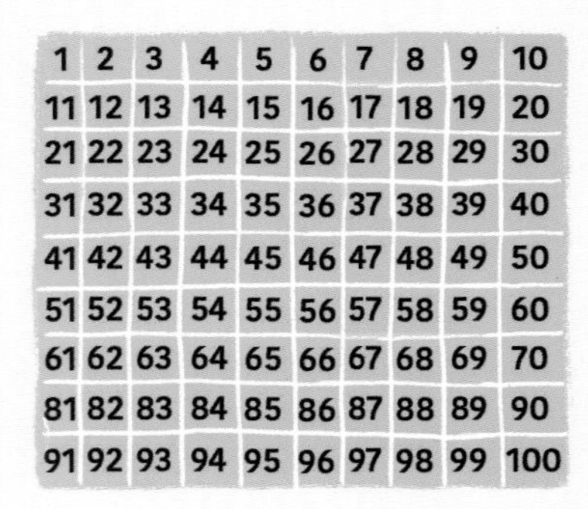

Rainstorm
This edition published by Parragon Books Ltd in 2018 and distributed by:
Parragon Inc. • 440 Park Avenue South, 13th Floor • New York, NY 10016, U.S.A. • 
Written by Joseph T. Garcia • Illustrated by Chris Jevons • Edited by Sarah Bradshaw • Designed by Emmy Reis • Production by Danielle Angell • Prepress by Michael Penman
 • Printed in China • ISBN 978-1-5270-0274-6

# Tommy Tummy Ache

Joseph T. Garcia

Chris Jevons

For the mother who carried me,
and was always there without fail.
And for the father who taught me,
that a poem could tell a tale.

JTG

Tommy
Tummy Ache
Joseph T. Garcia
Chris Jevons

In a little red school,
by a little blue lake,
sat a very clever boy,
named Tommy Tummy Ache.

Some students learn slow,
while others learn quick.
Tommy learned very fast,
to pretend he was sick.

Tommy hated school,
there was nothing worse.
So he'd fake an illness
and be sent to the nurse.

Tommy never did homework,
and rarely took a test.
Grammar was boring,
math a horrid pest.

His teacher was doubtful,
he could tell by her looks.
He knew he had to be creative,
so he studied medical books.

Tommy faked the measles,

and a case of the mumps,

he even made up an ailment,

that gave his skin lumps.

Sometimes he'd have cramps,

sometimes he'd be sneezy,

often he'd be coughing,

but mostly just queasy.

Tommy mastered fake illness,
not a day did he skip.
He had it all figured out,
until the big class trip.

They were off to Wild World,
to ride until dark.
No sickness planned today,
at the great amusement park!

Tommy flew off the bus,
right to the first attraction.
The Famous Flying Ferris Wheel,
with super-spinning action!

But his teacher blocked his way,
which made him uneasy.
She said he could not ride,
because he might get queasy.

The coaster was forbidden,
they really must be cautious.

With all the dips and drops,
Tommy would likely get nauseous.

No Ghost Mansion either,
they must show some restraint.
With all the scary monsters,
Tommy surely would faint.

The Falling Flume was nixed,
the water was just too freezing.
Because he'd had a cold,
Tommy might start sneezing.

His hopes of riding bumper cars,
Tommy's teacher quickly dashed.
With all his weakened muscles,
he'd likely get whiplash.

Tommy hid amid the crowd,
as they reached the Hurling Comet.
But alas his teacher found him,
fearful he would vomit.

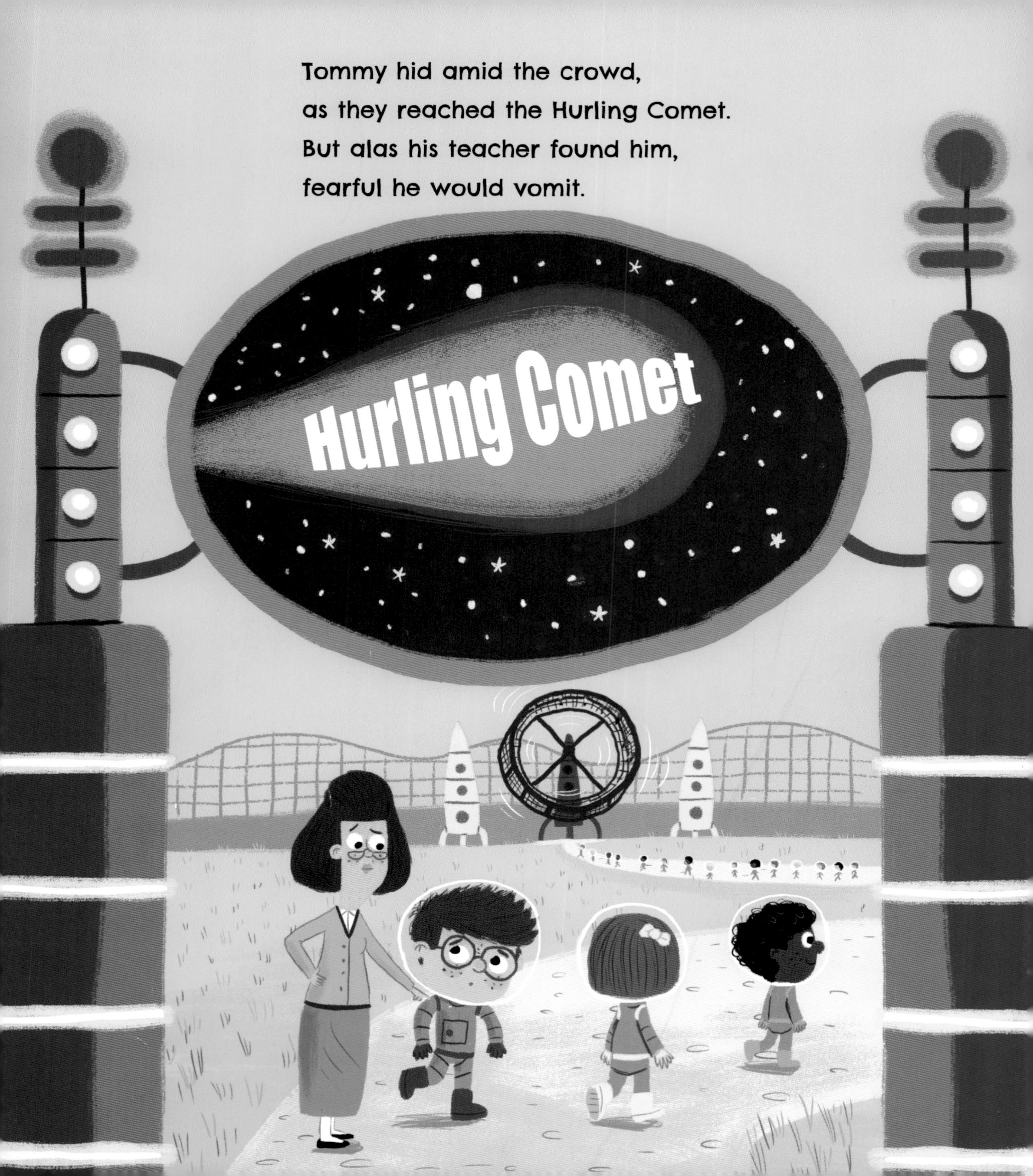

Ride after ride poor Tommy sat out,
the day was a complete mess.
He pleaded with his teacher,
but knew he must confess.

"Oh, Teacher, I'm so sorry,
I've been sly as a fox.
I was never really sick,
I'm healthy as an ox."

The teacher confessed also,
she'd known it all along.
But still he could not ride,
for faking sick was wrong.

Little Red
Lakeside School

"Tommy if you studied,
a great student you could be.
You only need to try,
work hard and you will see."

From then on Tommy studied,
and took each test like he should.
He stopped faking sickness,
and actually became quite good.

One last thing to point out,
before this story ends.
Little Tommy Tummy Ache
got his nickname from his friends.

Now in that small red school,
by the little blue lake,
sits a very bright boy,
called Tommy Timmy Blake.

The Wonderful World of Math!